Perfectly PETRA

By
AMBER HAYDEN DIXON

Perfectly PETRA

By
AMBER HAYDEN DIXON
ILLUSTRATED BY: L.M. PHANG

XULON PRESS ELITE

Xulon Press
2301 Lucien Way #415
Maitland, FL 32751
407.339.4217
www.xulonpress.com

Paperback ISBN-13: 978-1-6312-9888-2
Ebook ISBN-13: 978-1-6312-9889-9

FOR MY FAMILY,

MAY YOU ALWAYS KEEP YOUR FOCUS ON THE KINGDOM TO WHICH YOU BELONG.

I LOVE YOU.

The sun was shining and the clouds looked like cotton in the sky. The breeze felt nice. Petra felt as if she could fly. It was a beautiful, splendid, special sort of day. Petra felt certain nothing could get in her way. Leaving the palace to explore was such fun. Petra tufted her feathers and left her home in a run.

*P*etra set out to eat. *Mmm, insects and berries would be a nice snack.* As she pranced along, an olive branch hit her head with a smack. "Ow!" yelled Petra, as she tumbled over sticks and leaves. "I do not feel so well," she whispered, before she drifted off to sleep.

"Mooo-ve!" Petra was awakened by someone ordering in her ear. "Who am I? Where am I?" Petra asked, "How did I get here?" A cow looked down at her with displeasure on her face. "I don't want you here. You're not good enough. This field is a royal place." "I'm s-sorry," stammered Petra, taken aback by the cow's words. She couldn't remember...*Was that the meanest thing she had ever heard?*

Petra walked on sadly, still hungry for some lunch. She did not know who she was, but she must not be much.

It was not long before Petra came upon a river winding next to her path. She stopped and considered if she should step in for a bath. As she neared the crystal water, Petra sighed with great delight, but suddenly heard a, "Meow-over!" from a voice not so slight. "What are you doing?" A cat asked before he bent to clean his paw. He looked over Petra shrewdly and then licked his whiskered jaw. He slowly prowled over with a certain gleam in his eye. Petra did not know what to say. She did not want to lie.

"*I* wanted to look at the water. I considered taking a swim." "You can't touch that water," said the cat with a not-so-friendly grin. "Why ever not?" asked Petra. She was feeling unsure. "Because this river is clean," he said with a purr. "You're a silly, dirty bird and it would not be safe... to let someone like you swim in this special place."

*P*etra felt ashamed at his words. Was she dirty? Was she a silly bird? She couldn't remember...*Was that the meanest thing she had ever heard*?

Petra decided it was best to hurry up and go. She did not know who she was, but she must be pretty low.

*G*rrrr, *Grrrr, Grrrr*. She could hear her stomach rumble as she went on her way. *Swoosh, Swoosh, Swoosh* went her big feathers as she sashayed. "I can't focus on anything with my loud feathers and my grumbling tummy. I need to stop being a silly bird and find some berries—anything—yummy!"

*P*etra reached a grassy hill with a magnificent view. She could see a meadow, the river, and a beautiful castle too. She was filled with hope. "Oh my, a castle! What a lovely sight to see. I wonder if they have any food that they could spare for me."

Crunch, Crunch, Crunch. Petra heard eating from somewhere nearby. "Pssst. Down here," said a rat, trying to be sly. "I can get you some goods from the castle. No problem. Easy. I don't work for free though, you got it? Ka-peezy?" The rat looked at her expectantly as she considered what he said. Petra didn't trust him, but she needed to be fed. "How much should I pay, rat, for some fresh grain and water?" "Not much," said the rat. "Only one, single feather." "Would you please spare some nuts or pumpkin? You have some there, laying on a napkin." "This is my food," said the rat, quickly getting angry. "If I gave you half of my food, then we would *both* be hungry!"

*P*etra felt hungry, tired, and weary to the core. She told the rat she would pay him when he returned from his chore. He was not pleased with her idea, but eventually agreed. Before the rat left, Petra leaned back against an olive tree. "Yes, get some rest," crooned the rat. "While I find you a treat. It must be difficult walking with your furless, ugly feet." Petra thought that hurt her feelings. She frowned at her feet without any fur. She couldn't remember...*Was that the meanest thing she had ever heard?*

"Wake up!" Chirped a voice from somewhere up above. "You must rise now, child," urged a little, white dove. "What do you want from me?" Petra asked, tired and forlorn. "Are you here to criticize my feet, my beak, and lack of a horn? I know that I am a bird. I know the entire drill. I know that I am not good enough to sleep on this royal hill. I just want to eat, bathe, and feel free to be. I want to know my name and know that I am perfectly *ME!*"

"You are Petra, child. The castle in the distance is your home. You must believe. You are a peacock, a beautiful and cherished bird, indeed. Even better than that, you are The King's royal pet! There is only one of you, Petra. You are loved. Do not fret. I am a bird, too. Can't you see I am free? I see all the comings and goings from up in the trees."

*S*MACK! "Ow!" Petra exclaimed as she got up from her bed. A tree branch had fallen and bumped her on the head. "Wait a minute..." thought Petra, as she swayed to the thought. "I am Petra! I remember!" Then she took off in a trot.

"Thank you, little dove," Petra called back as she ran. She passed the rat carrying grain, berries, and ham. "Not today!" Petra called. The rat looked bewildered. Petra smiled as she realized that her feathers were treasured.

_P_etra passed the cat laying by the sparkling river. This time, the gleam in his eye didn't cause a shiver.

_S_he skipped and swayed and fluttered her quills. She ran past the cow standing in the field. "Hello, cow! Best of luck to you! I'm going home to see The King. So long, Toodle-oo!

"Oh, Petra," said The King when she made it to the throne. "I was worried you were gone for good. What courage you have shown! I hope you know how special you are. You are such a glorious bird."

Petra now remembered…

31

32

That hat was the nicest thing she had ever heard.

Lightning Source UK Ltd.
Milton Keynes UK
UKRC010954240820
368740UK00001B/4